Su-Su grinned to herself.

Tongue-Tied didn't know it, but she had just become the first student in Su-Su McCarthy's School of Flirting!

As soon as she got home, Su-Su dug out the magazine with the article on flirting and listed all the tips it gave in the back of her notebook.

1. Make eye contact.
2. Act happy and self-confident.
3. Use positive body language.
4. Give him compliments.
5. Show genuine interest in him.
6. Ask him questions to get a conversation started.
7. Be a good listener.
8. Remember that some boys are shy, too, and won't make the first move because they're scared of the big R word (rejection!)

Wow, thought Su-Su as she read through the list again. This was going to be a tougher job than she had originally thought...

Listen in on all the BOY TALK!

And coming soon:

#5
TONGUE-TIED

by Betsy Haynes

BULLSEYE BOOKS

Random House 🏠 New York

For Helen Meyer with much affection

Chapter One

"Hey, guys, listen to this!" Su-Su McCarthy looked up from the magazine lying open in front of her in the sand. "'Breaking the ice is the first step to melting his heart.' Isn't that romantic? I just read it in this article."

Her two best friends, Joni Sparkman and Crystal Britton, were stretched out on beach towels on either side of her. Joni had her nose in a Lindsey Jones mystery novel, and Crystal was lying on her back, eyes closed, listening to music through headphones. It was a Tuesday, which was normally a school day, but the teachers at Sunshine Beach Middle School had a conference day. The girls, all seventh graders, had opted for a day on the beautiful Florida beach.

"You don't need to break the ice with Chris," Crystal said without opening her eyes. "He's already your boyfriend."

"Yeah," said Joni. "What's the big deal? You aren't planning on going out with some other guy, are you?"

"Hey, no big deal," Su-Su said, feeling a little miffed. Her friends seemed unmoved by something so beautiful and poetic—not to mention so true. So what if she and Chris Oberlin were going out together and he was the most gorgeous, humongously wonderful boy in school? That didn't mean she couldn't do a little harmless flirting. He wouldn't have to know. Besides, the article she was reading on the art of flirting made it sound like so much fun.

Su-Su gazed out across the crowded beach toward the beautiful blue water of the Gulf of Mexico.

Of course she and Joni and Crystal didn't always agree on everything, even though they were best friends. Joni had short, dark hair that looked windblown most of the time. She planned to be a mystery writer someday, and patterned practically her entire life after Lindsey Jones, the heroine of her favorite mystery series. Even though Joni turned up her nose at horoscopes, Su-Su thought her friend was a typical Scorpio. Witty and independent, Joni loved anything mysterious. On the negative side, she could be suspicious sometimes, and she had a major potential for jealousy.

Just ask her boyfriend, Su-Su thought, chuckling to herself. Joni and Beau Maguire were always squabbling.

Crystal Britton was true to her star sign, too: Cancer. Tenderhearted and kind, she always offered a shoulder to cry on to anyone who needed it. Of course she also took things much too seriously and was awfully gullible sometimes, but that was normal for a Cancer. Crystal was one of the smallest girls in their class. She had long, honey-blond hair and a dimple that appeared like magic in her left cheek whenever she smiled. And the person who made her smile the most was Evan Byrnes, her next-door neighbor and boyfriend.

Su-Su, who was named for both of her grandmothers, Susan and Suzanna, considered herself an expert on people. She loved being a Gemini. It was the sign of the Twins, and it was easy for her to be two people at once. Or three or four, for that matter. She loved being onstage, and shy had never been a word used to describe her. Of course some people accused her of being fickle and of manipulating others the way some Geminis did, but that was only because they didn't really know her. She was also happy enough with her looks—tall with long, flaming red hair and outrageous clothes. She knew those were the things that set her apart.

Although the three girls didn't always agree with one another, there was one very important thing they definitely had in common: Boy Talk, the romance advice hot line they had set up in secret on Crystal's father's answering machine.

Every afternoon for an hour after school, kids from all over town called in to record their problems on the answering machine or to listen to other kids' recordings and offer their advice. The best part was that no one suspected Su-Su, Joni, and Crystal were behind it.

Su-Su glanced at her watch and frowned. They would have to leave the beach pretty soon. It was two o'clock already, and Boy Talk started at three-thirty. Even though there was no school, Boy Talk was still on because it was a weekday. If she was going to try out all these terrific flirting tips at the beach today, she'd better get started. But first she would have to pick a victim.

She sat up, put on sunglasses to hide her eyes, and began scoping out the males in the area. This was going to be fun. But as she looked around, she sighed with disappointment. Most of the guys were either too old or too young. A lot of the cute boys were with girls. And the boys who weren't with the girls weren't cute. She certainly had no intention of flirting with just *anyone*.

Su-Su turned her attention to a group of kids playing volleyball in the sand. They were all about the right age, and there was a mix of boys and girls, most of them boys. Among the girls, she recognized Megan Scully and Kim Scarborough. Kim was usually shy, but she was playing a great game of volleyball, spiking the ball over the net like a pro. Su-Su didn't know any of the guys, even though a couple of them looked kind of familiar. She carefully looked them over. Nope, too geeky, too young looking, too slobby. Too...*incredible!*

Her eyes fastened onto a bronze face set with brilliant blue eyes. His hair was sun-bleached blond, and he had an easy, confident smile.

Wow! Su-Su thought. Then a stab of guilt struck her. She really did care about her boyfriend Chris—a lot. This guy didn't mean a thing to her. It would be just a little harmless flirting, a little innocent fun.

Before she could lose her nerve, she scanned the list of tips in the magazine once again. Make eye contact. Act happy and self-confident. Use positive body language. Give him compliments. Show genuine interest in him. There it was! The ideal tip. *Show genuine interest in him.* She didn't have to read any farther.

Su-Su hugged her knees impatiently. She would wait until the game was over, then saunter over to him, acting totally casual and cool. She'd pretend she didn't know anything about volleyball and ask him to explain the game.

It's a great plan, Su-Su told herself. Naturally this gorgeous guy would be flattered and think she was terrific. Breaking the ice was the first step to melting his heart, just like the article said. She pulled a brush and mirror out of her beach bag and gave herself a quick once-over.

I'm ready, she thought.

She watched from behind her dark sunglasses as the game finally broke up.

"Be back in a minute, guys," she told her friends. She got to her feet and headed toward the bench by the volleyball net, where the kids were picking up their things and starting to walk away in different directions.

Su-Su caught her breath, her heart pounding with excitement. He had slung his beach towel around his neck and was reaching for a soda can sitting in the sand as she came up. Just as her shadow crossed his outstretched arm, he looked up.

She pasted a big smile on her face. "Hi," she said.

Suddenly she was terrified. Was that her natural voice, or had the word come out as a squeak? Would he say hi back or would he ignore her? Or worse, would he think she was a total idiot?

"Hi," he said, a slow smile spreading over his face. "How's it going?"

Su-Su's pulse jolted into high gear. "Great. How about you?" she asked. This time her voice came out loud and clear.

"Everything's cool," he said, and stood up. "See you around, okay?" Su-Su was sure from the way he said it that he was hoping he really *would* see her around.

He took a deep swig of his soda and started walking toward the parking lot.

Su-Su watched him go, feeling as if she would explode any second. She had flirted before, of course, but only as an untrained amateur. With a bit of luck and that magazine article she was on her way to becoming an expert. She hadn't actually gotten around to asking him anything about volleyball, but that didn't matter. She had gotten his attention. There was nothing to flirting if you kept your cool. And best of all, it was fun!

Chapter Two

"Who was that cute guy you were talking to just before we left the beach?" asked Crystal as she, Joni, and Su-Su were putting the Boy Talk tape into the answering machine at Crystal's house a little while later.

"You weren't flirting with him, were you?" Joni asked suspiciously.

"Of course not," Su-Su said, acting as if it were the furthest thing from her mind. At the same time, she hated herself for lying to her best friends. "We just said hi to each other, that's all."

Joni gave her a skeptical look. "Oh, yeah? You had to get up and go all the way over to the volleyball net just to say hi to a perfect stranger right after you read an article on flirting? Ex-*cuse* me, but I don't think so."

Su-Su was grateful that the phone on the answering machine rang before she had to lie again. Crystal and Joni just didn't understand the first thing about harmless flirting. But she, Su-Su, understood. In fact, with a little more practice, she just might open a school for flirting.

"Hello, welcome to Boy Talk," said the greeting on the tape. Su-Su had recorded it in a fake English accent so that none of the girls who called in would recognize her voice. "Thank you ever so much for ringing up." The tape went on to explain how to leave a message after the beep or to punch 1 to hear all the messages other callers had recorded.

Beep.

"Hi, Boy Talk. I have a serious problem. I'm only thirteen, but I'm in love with Brad Pitt. My friends think I'm crazy. I've seen all his movies and I can't live without him! I've sent him four fan letters, but so far he hasn't answered a single one. What am I going to do? Don't tell me to get real. *I can't!* Call me Crazy Crush."

"Brad Pitt!" Su-Su shrieked. "She really is crazy if she thinks she can get Brad Pitt interested in her by sending him fan letters. He probably gets thousands of fan letters a week from love-struck girls."

"Don't make fun of her," scolded Crystal. "Poor kid. She's really hurting."

"Yeah, but Brad Pitt?" Joni shook her head. "That girl's got the wrong name. She should have called herself Hopeless."

"Well, I can sympathize with her," said Crystal. "I sort of know how she feels. I remember when nobody thought I'd ever have a chance with Evan because he was going out with Alison Hamel." She lifted her chin. "I guess I showed them."

"That's different," said Su-Su. "You two live next door to each other. You could at least communicate with him. He knew you were alive. You could even flirt!"

The phone rang again.

Beep.

"I hope somebody's listening who can help me, because I don't know what to do. I've been stood up twice by this guy I really like, but he's always had an excuse. Last night he called and asked me out for the third time. I stalled because I don't know if I can trust him not to stand me up again. Should I give him one more chance or tell him to buzz off? Call me Tough Choice."

"I don't blame her for being worried," said Joni. "He sounds like a real jerk to me."

"Not necessarily," said Crystal. "Maybe his other excuses were real."

"Oh, right," scoffed Joni. "He's probably bragging to his friends about how he has this girl wrapped around his little finger and how he can stand her up and then call her and she'll jump at the chance to go out."

"Where do you guys get these weirdos like Crazy Crush, anyway? It just proves that this whole stupid Boy Talk thing is a fake. Nobody—I mean *nobody* would fall for a dumb call like that!" The receiver was slammed down so hard that Su-Su, Crystal, and Joni all three jumped.

Su-Su drew in her breath. "That was April Mathis!"

"We haven't heard from her in ages. I thought maybe she'd given up trying to wreck Boy Talk," said Crystal.

Joni narrowed her eyes. "Don't kid yourself. She's just been keeping quiet so we'd *think* she'd given up. This call proves it. She's probably been listening all along, just waiting for the right moment to pounce."

Crystal looked worried. "Do you think she'll convince people that Boy Talk is fake? I mean, it isn't! All the girls who call in really need help with their problems."

Su-Su gazed off into the distance and thought about April Mathis. The girl was captain of the cheerleading squad and the leader of the most popular clique at Sunshine Beach Middle School. She hated Boy Talk because she didn't want anything or anyone getting more attention at school than she did. She was also determined to find out who was behind the hot line, which made Su-Su, Joni, and Crystal very nervous. The whole thing could be ruined if people calling in found out Boy Talk was being run by kids they knew.

The ringing of the phone brought Su-Su back to the present.

Beep.

"Hi, Boy Talk. This is a message for Crazy Crush. I was glad to hear your message because I know exactly how you feel! I'm in love with Keanu Reeves! I had to send him fourteen fan letters before I got a postcard back with his autograph, but it was worth it. I need advice as much as you do, so I'll be listening. Call me Crazy Crush, Too."

"Oh, great," muttered Su-Su. "If April hears that, she'll laugh her head off."

"What if that last call wasn't real?" asked Joni. "What if April Mathis put one of her clones up to it? It could be her latest plot to destroy Boy Talk."

"Uh-oh, you could be right," Crystal said in a worried voice. "Maybe both of those calls were fake."

Su-Su was worried about that too. And the last thing she needed was to be distracted by April Mathis just now. She wanted to concentrate on her flirting techniques.

The phone rang again.

At first there was nothing but dead silence on the tape. Then Su-Su heard someone clear her throat. "Um,…Boy Talk? I…I… Oh, gosh, I can't do this."

The receiver clicked, leaving only the sound of the dial tone.

Chapter Three

"I wonder what *her* problem was," said Joni.

Su-Su shrugged. "Who knows? Maybe she'll call back."

"I hope so," said Crystal, frowning. "She sounded as if she really needs help."

Calls poured in for the next few minutes, most just kids listening. One girl, calling herself On the Move, told Crazy Crush and Crazy Crush, Too, that she was trying to convince her parents to move to Hollywood so she could be closer to Ethan Hawke. A few other girls called to talk, but none of them seemed to be the mysterious caller.

Beep.

"Hi, Boy Talk, this is One More Chance. I have a message for Tough Choice. If he has enough nerve to call you again, he might be on the level. And what if you refuse him and find out later that he's a great guy? I think you should give him one more chance."

Beep.

"Tough Choice, if you're listening, take my advice. Drop him like a hot potato. It's obvious he's a jerk and he's using you. I know. I've been there. Just call me Been Jerked Around."

Beep.

"Hey, Tough Choice! What do you know about this guy, anyway? If you don't know much, ask around. Try to find out if he has a rotten track record with other girls. If he does, you're better off without him. And if you turn him down, then maybe he'll realize you're not somebody he can tromp all over, and he'll shape up. You'll also save your self-respect. Call me Checking Up."

When the phone rang at 4:25, Crystal gave a weary sigh and said, "This is definitely our last call of the day. I'm beat."

"You said it," agreed Su-Su.

Beep.

There was a pause. Then a meek-sounding voice said, "Hi, Boy Talk, I'm sorry I hung up before."

Su-Su, Joni, and Crystal snapped to attention.

"I've got a really embarrassing problem," she went on. "Every time the boy I like even says something simple like hi to me I just stand there staring at him like a jerk. What am I going to do? I guess a good name for me is Tongue-Tied." She sighed sadly and then hung up.

"Poor Tongue-Tied," said Crystal. "It must be awful to freeze up like that."

Su-Su screwed her face into a frown. "I've heard that voice before," she mused. She stared at the ceiling for a minute. "I could be wrong, but wasn't that Kim Scarborough?"

"You mean that girl who was at our gym class last year? The one who turned beet-red every time she had to change her clothes in front of everybody in the locker room?" asked Joni.

"That's the one," said Su-Su. Kim had curly brown hair and a cute smile. But she kept her eyes turned downward most of the time and hardly ever talked to anybody. "She's nice," said Su-Su. "But boy, is she shy. Except," she corrected, "when she plays volleyball."

"I sure hope someone calls in tomorrow with some good advice for her," said Crystal. "How do you explain to somebody like that that boys won't bite?" she added.

A light flashed on in Su-Su's brain. "What did you just say, Crystal?"

"I said, how do you explain to somebody like Kim Scarborough that boys don't bite," Crystal repeated. "Why?"

"Oh, nothing," murmured Su-Su, but her mind was starting to race at a million miles an hour. Tongue-Tied didn't know it, but she was about to become the first student in Su-Su McCarthy's School of Flirting!

As soon as she got home, Su-Su dug out the magazine with the article on flirting from her beach bag and listed all the tips it gave in the back of her notebook.

1. Make eye contact.
2. Act happy and self-confident.
3. Use positive body language.
4. Give him compliments.
5. Show genuine interest in him.
6. Ask him questions to get a conversation started.
7. Be a good listener.
8. Remember that some boys are shy, too. Sometimes they won't make a first move because they're scared of the big R word (rejection!).

Hmm, thought Su-Su as she read through the list again. This was going to be a tougher job than she had originally thought. If Tongue-Tied had mega anxiety attacks whenever the boy she liked said hi, how was she, Su-Su, ever going to teach her to flirt?

Even getting Tongue-Tied to use the first tip, "Make eye contact," was going to be a major challenge.

But Su-Su was up to it.

Chapter Four

"Okay, let's see if we can find Kim Scarborough," Su-Su said the next morning when she, Joni, and Crystal met at school before class.

Crystal looked surprised. "Why?"

"So we can check her out and make sure she's really Tongue-Tied. You know, see if she acts shy around guys, stuff like that," Su-Su replied.

"Hey, wait a minute, Su-Su," Joni said in alarm. "You're not planning on getting involved, are you? If you are, you can count me out. I learned my lesson with Double Dumped."

"I'm not planning to get involved," Su-Su assured her.

She winced at her own words. That wasn't exactly true. In fact, she *did* plan to get involved, and she hated it that she'd just told her best friends another lie. But it was for a good cause, she reminded herself. Kim Scarborough needed help, and Su-Su knew she was the person who could help her.

"Isn't that her over there?" said Crystal. She was pointing to a girl with curly brown hair who was walking up the sidewalk toward school. Her eyes were trained downward, and she was alone. The girl passed two groups of girls, standing around waiting for the first bell without saying hi or even looking up.

"That's Kim, all right," said Su-Su, sighing. "And she definitely isn't Miss Congeniality."

"She must be Tongue-Tied," said Joni.

"I wonder who this guy is who's making her freeze up?" asked Crystal.

"Well, if we keep an eye on her, we might be able to figure that out," Su-Su said. "If we know who the guy is, we might know what to tell her to do."

"Su-Su, I'm warning you," Joni said angrily. "Stay out of this. Let somebody else give her advice. That's why we have Boy Talk, remember?"

Su-Su wanted to argue that it wasn't the only reason they had started the hot line. Sometimes they were able to get advice for their own problems, and besides, it was intriguing to listen in on other girls' romantic troubles and to try to figure out what they should do. She kept quiet, though. She didn't want to get into a fight with Joni. Besides, her horoscope this morning had said that her big mouth could get her into a lot of trouble if she didn't watch out. That meant she'd have to keep an eye on Kim on the sly.

She had just left her locker and was heading for her first-period class when she spotted Chris waiting for her by the drinking fountain.

Just looking at him practically took her breath away. Chris was definitely gorgeous. She loved the way his dark, wavy hair was casually brushed back off his face. His deep-set dark eyes gave him a mysterious look sometimes. But it was his smile that she loved best. She had never seen him without the same little sideways grin that he was wearing now. The only negative thing about him that she could think of was that his best friend was her older brother and constant tormentor, Patrick.

"Hey, Su-Su, what's happening?" Chris called out when she got near.

"I'll never tell," she said, giving him a flirty smile. "What about you?"

Chris shrugged as he fell in step beside her. "Not much. Patrick wants me to go to a ball game with him Friday night, but I'd rather be with you…if you want to do something."

"Sure, let's do something," Su-Su answered, hoping her face wasn't as red as her hair. She was still getting used to having a boyfriend, and it always discombobulated her when Chris asked her out.

"Cool," he said, his little sideways smile getting bigger.

Suddenly Su-Su remembered the flirting tips. Here was her perfect chance to practice. Now what were they? She racked her brain. *Use positive body language.* Whatever that meant. How could she even try to figure that out when she was walking though a crowded hall carrying an armload of books?

Make eye contact. She had already done that. *Give him compliments.*

Yikes! thought Su-Su. *What can I say? You have the cutest smile of any boy in the world? Just looking at you makes my knees turn to jelly? Help!*

Su-Su took a deep, calming breath. What was the next tip? *Show genuine interest in him.* Well, that wouldn't be hard. She'd never been so genuinely interested in a boy in her whole life. She wanted to know every single thing about Chris. What was his favorite color? Which bands did he like? What kind of pizza did he like best? But how could she ask him those things without sounding like Twenty Questions?

Just then Chris stopped in the middle of the hallway. "Well, here's my class. Catch you later, okay? I'll call you tonight, and we can decide what to do Friday."

"Right," Su-Su said. She gave a sigh of relief as

Chris went into the classroom. She was off the hook. This flirting business was a lot harder than it looked.

Su-Su was about to continue down the hall to her own class when she felt someone watching her. Glancing quickly back into the room, she blinked in surprise.

Someone was watching her, all right. It was the boy she had flirted with at the beach the day before. The blond guy with the dark tan and the gorgeous blue eyes. And he wasn't just glancing her way. His head was cocked to one side as if he were looking her over and liking what he saw. And he was giving her a huge grin.

Su-Su darted a glance at Chris to see if he had noticed, but he hadn't. His back was to her as he headed for his seat.

The blond boy was still smiling at her. He was so cute, and she didn't even know his name.

Su-Su couldn't help it. She shot a fast smile back at him as she raced off down the hall.

Chapter Five

Su-Su couldn't get the blond boy's flirtatious smile out of her mind for the rest of the day. Part of the time her face flamed with guilt at the though of flirting with another boy behind Chris's back. But other times she found herself wondering what he was really like and if he would be fun on a date.

I only went up to him at the beach and said hello, she thought in amazement. Had that been enough to break the ice like the article said? Was his heart actually starting to melt? The idea made her shiver with excitement. Maybe she was better at flirting than she realized. In that case she could definitely help Tongue-Tied. In fact the little bit of harmless flirting she had been doing was simply research for a good cause.

She could hardly wait to get to Boy Talk after school. "I'm going to record a message for Tongue-Tied," she announced as soon as the tape was in the answering machine. She held her breath and waited for Joni's reaction.

"You'll be sorry," Joni said, looking exasperated.

"I think it's sweet of you to want to help her, Su-Su," said Crystal. "But don't forget how careful we have to be not to let anyone figure out who we are. Especially now that April Mathis is out to get us again."

"I know, I know," Su-Su said impatiently. "It's just that I really think I can give Tongue-Tied some great advice."

"I agree with Crystal," said Joni. "I don't think you should do it."

Su-Su snorted in frustration. How could she make her friends see that they were wrong?

Just then the first call of the day came in.

Beep.

"Boy Talk, this is a message for Tongue-Tied. Ask a friend to call him and tell him that you like him but you're too shy to tell him yourself. As soon as he knows, he might ask you out. It's worth a try. Call me Wise One."

"What!" shrieked Su-Su. "That's the stupidest thing I ever heard. He'll know she's chasing him. Boys hate that. If Tongue-Tied takes Wise One's advice, she'll scare him off."

"I agree," said Joni. "I guess there's no way we can guarantee that everyone who calls Boy Talk is going to give good advice."

"Yeah, but—" Su-Su sputtered.

The phone was ringing again.

Beep.

"Hi, Boy Talk. I'd like to leave a message for Tongue-Tied. Don't worry if you're too shy to talk to the guy you like. If you can't say it, write it down. Send him a note telling him you like him. It's that simple. Call me The Write Stuff and spell it W-R-I-T-E. Get it?"

"Yeah, do we ever get it," said Joni, frowning. "And what if he's the kind of guy who'd humiliate Tongue-Tied by showing the note to all his friends? The Write Stuff is dead wrong."

"Don't you see? That's why I have to record a message myself," pleaded Su-Su. "I've practically memorized that article on flirting, and I can explain everything so it won't sound so scary. The tips really work, believe me."

Whoops! she thought as soon as she saw the surprised looks on Joni's and Crystal's faces. "I mean, they sound like they would work," she added quickly, trying to look as innocent as she could.

"It would be awful if the only advice Tongue-Tied got was from Wise One and The Write Stuff," said

Crystal. "She could mess up so badly that she'd be afraid of guys for life."

"That's what I'm saying," insisted Su-Su. "And that's why it's so important for her to get my message."

"I guess you're right," Joni admitted. "Just be sure to disguise your voice, okay? We don't want to take any chances."

"Except I don't think you should use any weird voices," said Crystal. "Tongue-Tied sounds real sensitive, and she might think you were making fun of her. That would be awful."

"Good point," said Su-Su, nodding.

She pulled out her list of flirting tips and studied them carefully. Kim was definitely sensitive. Su-Su knew she would have to approach her just right.

Su-Su could vaguely hear the sound of the Boy Talk phone ringing in the other room and the greeting coming on, but she couldn't let herself listen. She had to concentrate on helping Tongue-Tied. She made notes on possible things to say. Some of the tips were too complicated. Others took too much nerve.

Finally she was ready. Su-Su cocked an ear and listened. The Boy Talk line was free. She took a deep breath and punched in the hot line's number.

"Hello, welcome to Boy Talk," the greeting began. Su-Su drummed her nails on Crystal's desk and listened to her own fake English accent go through the instructions. Finally the beep sounded.

"Hi, Boy Talk. This is a message for Tongue-Tied," she said before she could lose her nerve. "I know how hard it is sometimes to be cool around the guy you like. Believe me, I've been there. But there's one thing you have to remember: Breaking the ice is the first step to melting his heart."

Su-Su paused to let the words sink in before she went on. "There are lots of things you can do to break the ice, but you should probably concentrate on just a few to start with."

"Pssst! Su-Su!"

Out of the corner of her eye, Su-Su could see Joni in the doorway. Her friend was frowning and waving her hands as if she wanted Su-Su to stop talking.

Su-Su ignored her. Joni could be such a pain sometimes.

"First, look him straight in the eye, smile, and say hello. That's all you have to do, and it only takes a second. Besides, it's almost a hundred percent certain that he'll say hi back," she said. "Trust me. It's easy and—"

"Su-Su! Hang up! Right now!"

This time it was Crystal trying to get her attention. Su-Su frowned at her friend, who was staring at her with horror written all over her face.

Putting her hand over the mouthpiece, Su-Su said

impatiently, "I'll be off in a minute."

"Sorry, Tongue-Tied," she said into the receiver. "What I wanted to say is, it really works. Just try it. Then call in again, and I'll tell you what to do next." Su-Su was about to hang up when she remembered something important. "Just call me Icebreaker," she said happily.

She hung up and looked toward the door. Joni and Crystal were both standing there staring at her. Their faces looked like storm clouds.

"Do you realize what you've done?" Joni demanded.

"Of course I do," Su-Su said defensively. "I've just given Tongue-Tied some terrific advice. What's your problem?"

"It's *your* problem, too. Especially if April Mathis was listening," said Crystal.

Su-Su frowned. She still didn't get it. Joni sighed deeply. "You blew it, Su-Su. You were so carried away with giving Tongue-Tied advice that you forgot to disguise your voice."

Chapter Six

As if Su-Su didn't already have enough on her mind, her brother Patrick decided to get on her case at suppertime.

"I hope you're happy now," he muttered around a bite of chicken and rice casserole that Su-Su had hastily defrosted and then heated in the microwave after their mother called to say she was working late. He gave Su-Su a surly look and dug his fork into his food again.

"Happy about what?" she asked. Deep down she had a feeling she didn't really want to know.

"About what?" Patrick mimicked in a high-pitched voice. "Chris Oberlin, that's what."

"That's *who*," Su-Su corrected, holding back a giggle. Patrick hated having his grammar corrected.

"So what about Chris, anyway? He seems fine to me."

Patrick put down his fork and glared at her. "That shows how much you know about guys."

Su-Su rolled her eyes in disgust. "So are you going to tell me what's bugging you or mercifully leave me in peace?" she asked.

"You're messing Chris up," said Patrick. "He was supposed to go to a ball game with *me* Friday night until you turned his brain to mush. Now all of a sudden he can't go to the game with me because he's got a hot date with you."

"Poor boy," crooned Su-Su. "Is itty-bitty Patrick going to have to go to the silly-willy ball game all by himself? Why don't you get a date, too? Or won't anybody go out with you?"

Su-Su ducked as Patrick hurled his balled-up paper napkin at her. He missed and stormed out of the kitchen.

It was Patrick's turn to clean up since she had fixed supper, but Su-Su shrugged to herself and carried the dirty dishes to the sink. She wanted to be by herself to think about what her brother had just let slip. Chris had already made plans to go to the game with Patrick when he decided to ask her to a movie instead! That might mean Chris was a lot more serious about their relationship than she had ever dreamed. Was he going to ask her not to date anyone else sometime soon? *Not that I'm planning to any-way*, Su-Su told herself. Chris was the only guy she wanted.

Su-Su could hardly believe her horoscope the next morning.

GEMINI (*May 21-June 20*) *Today could defi-nitely be your blissed-out day! Developments in an important relationship may have your heart singing. Communications are at the top of your agenda!*

She read it over two or three times before she left for school, trying to figure out exactly what it meant. Was this the day that Chris was going to ask her not to date anyone else? Was he going to tell her he hung around with Patrick just to be near her, the way she kept hoping he would? *Or maybe my horo-scope has something to do with the gorgeous blond guy I was practicing flirting on*, she thought with a stab of guilt.

This was going to be an interesting day.

"I bet the communications part means April Mathis recognized your voice and she's making plans to expose Boy Talk," Joni said when Su-Su read her horoscope to Joni and Crystal.

Su-Su was flabbergasted. "What? This has nothing to do with April Mathis! Didn't you hear the first part? It says this will be a blissed-out day."

"Maybe it doesn't have anything to do with April or you," Crystal said thoughtfully. "Maybe it's talking about Tongue-Tied. It would make you happy if you found out she got your message, took your advice, and got the boy she likes to notice her, right?"

"Well...yes...I guess so," said Su-Su, feeling deflated. It wasn't that she didn't want Tongue-Tied to learn how to attract guys, but she certainly didn't want to read about it in her own personal horoscope. And she didn't like the way Joni brought up April, either, reminding her that she'd forgotten to disguise her voice when she called Boy Talk yesterday. She hadn't forgotten on purpose. What was the matter with everybody?

"Look, there's Kim Scarborough over there," said Joni, pointing toward the front of the school.

Su-Su turned around to see Kim walking slowly up the front steps.

"And look, there's a boy walking toward her!" said Crystal.

"Don't let her see us watching," said Joni. "That might be the guy she likes." Su-Su slipped on her sunglasses so she could watch Kim without being noticed. This could be Tongue-Tied's big moment, and Su-Su didn't want to miss it.

Suddenly Kim glanced up and saw the boy. She stopped in her tracks and abruptly whirled around, was beet-red as she hurried across the grass and ducked behind a pink bougainvillea bush in the center of the school ground.

"Oh, no!" wailed Su-Su. "Did you see that? She just missed her big chance."

Crystal sighed and gave Su-Su a sheepish grin. "I guess your horoscope wasn't talking about Tongue-Tied after all."

Su-Su figured Joni would make another remark about April, but instead her friend was gazing toward the pink bougainvillea bush where Kim was hiding.

"You know, that girl really needs mega help," Joni said. "She's even too shy to say hi."

"Hmm," Crystal said. "There has to be some way we can help her if we really try. If we could just…" She shrugged helplessly as her voice trailed off. "I don't know *what* we can do except hope that some great advice will come through on Boy Talk for her. Any brilliant new suggestions?"

Su-Su was still watching the boy sauntering up the sidewalk. He didn't seem to notice that Kim had disappeared into thin air. He probably doesn't even know she exists, Su-Su thought.

"He looks familiar," said Su-Su. She squinted and gave the boy a closer look. He was sort of cute, with dark, unruly hair and big sad cocker-spaniel eyes. "I think I know him from somewhere."

"Yeah, he looks familiar to me, too," said Crystal. "

"Yeah, he looks familiar to me, too," said Crystal. "

"His name's David Spiegel," said Joni. "His picture was in the newspaper a few weeks ago, remember?"

Su-Su kept on staring at him. It took her a minute to remember the picture. Then it dawned on her. "I remember now!" she said. "There was an article about all the time he spends helping out with the Special Olympics. No wonder Kim Scarborough thinks he's special."

She watched until David disappeared inside the school. There had to be some way she and her friends could help Kim. She opened her mouth to tell Joni and Crystal the idea that had just popped into her mind and then caught herself.

It's my idea, she told herself. *And I'm the only one who can carry it off. Besides, they probably wouldn't go along with it anyway.*

Su-Su smiled to herself. Her horoscope had been right. Communications were going to be at the top of her agenda.

Chapter Seven

Su-Su was so lost in thought over her plan to help Kim that she didn't notice someone come up behind her as she left her locker and headed for her first-period class.

"Hi, how's it going?"

She looked around and almost jumped out of her skin. It was *him*—the guy from the beach. His blond hair shone like gold in the morning sunlight, and his blue eyes sparkled as he smiled at her.

"Oh, hi!" she said breathlessly. She hoped she didn't look as dazed as she sounded. "Great," she added, giving him a quick smile. "Um, how about you?"

His smile grew wider. "Everything's cool. You know, I see you around school a lot, and I don't even know your name."

Su-Su's heart felt all fluttery. This gorgeous guy actually wanted to know her name! Her flirting techniques were working! This was the perfect time to try another of the tips she had read in the magazine, but her mind was a complete blank, and he was waiting for an answer.

"It's Su-Su McCarthy," she said, even though it took every bit of nerve she had. "The Su-Su stands for Susan Suzanna. I know it's a weird name, but they were my grandmothers."

"I don't think it's weird. I like it," he said. "My name's pretty boring. Brian Ferguson."

Su-Su wanted to tell him she didn't think his name was plain and she really liked it, too, but instead she glanced at him shyly and said, "Hi, Brian."

He gave her the same approving look he had given her the morning before when she'd stopped outside the door to Chris's first period-class and seen Brian sitting inside.

Chris!

The thought of her boyfriend shot through her like an electric current, almost choking off her breath. What would he think if he walked up right now and saw her talking to Brian? Would he suspect she was flirting and get mad? Would he break their date and tell her to get lost?

But it's only research! Another part of her brain shouted. *I'm doing this for Kim!*

Su-Su bit her bottom lip. She really should do a little more research. For Kim, of course. She still hadn't tried the tip about showing a genuine interest in him.

"So do you play a lot of volleyball?" she asked brightly. "It looks like fun, but I've never actually played. I don't even know the rules."

"Hey, it's a blast," Brian said eagerly. "I play at the beach two or three times a week after school. Weekends, too. Lots of kids from school play. You should come along sometime and I'll teach you the game. How about it?"

"Well..." Su-Su hesitated. It hadn't occurred to her that he might invite her to play. "Sure, maybe sometime," she said.

Mercifully they started walking. Brian nodded toward a corridor they were about to pass. "My class is down there," he said. "But I'll see you around, okay?"

All Su-Su could do was nod. She moved on toward her own class like a zombie. *It's too incredible to be true*, she thought. After all this time of not being able to get a date with anybody, suddenly she had hit the jackpot. Not only did she have the boy of her dreams for a boyfriend, but after only a few quick moments of flirting, another gorgeous guy was interested in her, too.

This was definitely one blissed-out day.

Su-Su was dying to tell Joni and Crystal about Brian Ferguson when she got to the cafeteria at noon. She was desperate to tell somebody—*anybody*—about him. But she knew she had better keep her mouth shut.

Joni would immediately think she was cheating on Chris, which of course she wasn't. Crystal was a diehard romantic, so she might be a little more sympathetic. She probably wouldn't go so far as to believe Su-Su was practicing her flirting to help Tongue-Tied, though. Of course, Su-Su reminded herself, she had an even bigger plan to help Tongue-Tied, but she had to keep it a secret for now. That left her exactly nothing to talk about to her friends.

"How come you're so quiet today?" Joni asked her as the three of them munched their sandwiches.

"Yeah," said Crystal, her eyes twinkling. "I thought this was supposed to be your blissed-out day."

"Me, too," Su-Su said and shrugged. "Oh well."

"Don't worry yet. It's only noon," Crystal said. "There's a lot more left of today."

Su-Su nodded and glanced over Crystal's shoulder.

Kim Scarborough had just left the cashier with her lunch tray Now she was walking slowly down an aisle, looking around the crowded lunchroom for someplace to sit. She didn't seem to notice that David Spiegel had stopped in the same aisle and was watching her approach.

"Hey, guys, check this out," Su-Su said, nodding in Kim's direction without taking her eyes off the girl.

"Wow, they're on a collision course for love," Crystal said dreamily. "I sure hope Kim follows your advice, Su-Su."

"She's crazy if she doesn't," Su-Su mumbled. "How hard can it be to look at someone and say hi?"

"How would you know? You've never been shy in your life," Joni teased.

Su-Su didn't answer. She kept her eyes glued on Kim. Any second now she would have to notice David. Su-Su crossed and uncrossed her fingers. Her advice had to work. If only Kim would give it a try.

Su-Su held her breath as Kim slowly raised her eyes. When she saw David, she stiffened and looked startled. Then she whirled around and took off in the opposite direction with her tray. David watched her go, looking confused.

"What's the matter with that girl?" Su-Su blurted . "That was her perfect chance. She blew it."

"She's just horribly, painfully shy," said Crystal.

"It reminds me of a Lindsey Jones mystery I read, *The Case of the Bashful Bank Robber*," said Joni. "The guy was so shy that he couldn't look at the teller when he asked her to hand over the money."

Su-Su was only half listening. She was too busy thinking about Kim. It was pretty obvious that there was no amount of advice anyone could leave on Boy Talk that would help poor Tongue-Tied get over her problem.

Su-Su knew she would have to jump into action and take care of things herself. And she planned to do it just as soon as she got home from Boy Talk.

Chapter Eight

The phone began ringing the moment Su-Su, Joni, and Crystal put the Boy Talk tape into the answering machine.

Beep.

"Hi, Boy Talk. I have a serious problem. I have this great boyfriend who says he loves me. The problem is, I'm not in love, I'm in like. He wants to get pre-engaged. I don't want to. I don't even know what that is! I really don't want to break up with him, but if I don't, will I be leading him on? Call me Only in Like."

"That's a new one," said Su-Su, shaking her head.

Crystal nodded sadly. "I think she should break up with him and look for a boyfriend she can really care about."

"She sounds pretty sensible to me," said Joni. "It's stupid to get totally carried away with every boy you date."

"Are you calling *me* carried away?" Crystal huffed.

"Of course not," said Joni. "I just meant—"

The ringing telephone interrupted her as more calls came in for Boy Talk.

Beep.

"Help, Boy Talk! My phone rings constantly. Every time I answer it, it's always the same boy. He likes me a lot, but I just don't like him. He bugs me to go out with him, but he won't take no for an answer. What can I do? Just call me No Way."

Beep.

"I sure hope you're listening, Boy Talk, because I have a huge problem on my hands. I've had a crush on somebody for ages. We finally went steady for a couple of weeks. Then he suddenly broke up with me. He won't even tell me why! I don't know what I did wrong. How can I find out and let him know how badly I want him back? Call me Sad and Confused."

The next few calls were from girls who wanted to listen, but before long the advice began pouring in.

Beep.

"Hi, Boy Talk. This is for No Way. Maybe your parents could help out. Ask them to answer the phone and tell him you're not available. It won't be a lie, because you really aren't available. *To him*, anyway. Sign me Not a Phone-y."

Beep.

"This is a message for Sad and Confused. If you've asked him why he broke up with you and he won't give you an answer, maybe it's because *he's* the one who is confused. He sounds immature to me. Why would you want a jerk like that back? My advice is the same as my name. Forget Him!"

"I like Forget Him's style," said Joni. She rubbed her hands together and grinned.

"Right," snorted Su-Su. "Then how come you let Beau get away with murder all the time? Remember when you caught him sneaking around? You talked big, but you were the biggest softie in the world."

Joni flashed her a sheepish look. "Can I help it if I'm not perfect?"

"Speaking of not perfect, I sure wish Tongue-Tied would call in again," said Su-Su. "I'm dying to know what she has to say for herself. How hard can it be to smile at a guy and say hi?"

Beep.

"Hi, Boy Talk. I just want to tell Sad and Confused not to be too hard on herself over why her boyfriend wanted to break up. It wasn't her fault. If she'd done something so bad that it made him want to call it quits, she'd know it. Listen up, Sad and Confused, and look around. The world is full of cute guys. Call me All Eyes."

Beep.

"This is a message for Only in Like. If you ask me, the word *love* is definitely overused. I mean, this guy would probably tell you he loves his skateboard and then say he loves you two minutes later. Relax. Being in like is cool. You're definitely not leading him on. Call me Likes Like."

Su-Su fidgeted and looked at her watch. It was almost four-thirty and time to shut down Boy Talk for the day. She couldn't get Tongue-Tied out of her mind.

Beep.

"Hi, Boy Talk. This is Tongue-Tied again."

"Finally!" cried Su-Su, snapping to attention.

"I tried to do what you said. You know, smile and say hi. But the second I looked at him my palms got all sweaty, my heart started pounding, and butterflies were zooming around in my stomach. I feel like such a failure. I guess there's no use trying anymore. I'm just going to give up."

"Don't you dare!" Su-Su shouted at the answering machine, even though she knew Tongue-Tied couldn't hear her. "You're not enrolled in Su-Su McCarthy's School of Flirting for nothing. I'm going to teach you how to get a boy's attention if it kills me."

"Su-Su McCarthy's School of Flirting?" Crystal

asked, screwing up her face in bewilderment. "What are you talking about?"

"Whoops," Su-Su said, biting her lip. She hoped she hadn't blown everything now. "I was just…you know…kidding," she said. She shrugged and tried to look innocent. "I'm positive she could get this guy to notice her if she followed the advice in that article. I'm going to call in again and give her a pep talk."

"Wait a minute," said Joni, holding up her hand. "You forgot to disguise your voice yesterday, remember? Maybe April put Tongue-Tied up to calling in today so she could hear your voice again."

"But Tongue-Tied is Kim Scarborough," argued Su-Su. "She doesn't hang around with April."

"Are you one hundred percent sure it's Kim?" asked Joni.

"Well, no, not exactly," Su-Su admitted. "But it sounds like her voice. And you saw how she acted yesterday around David Spiegel. It *has* to be Kim."

"Well, you have twenty-three hours to decide for sure if you want to call in again," said Crystal, flipping off the answering machine. "Boy Talk is over for today."

Su-Su sighed in resignation and gathered her books to head for home. *Fine*, she thought. *I'll just have to wait until tomorrow. But I'm definitely calling in.*

And in the meantime she was going to put the other part of her plan into action.

Chapter Ten

Su-Su could hardly wait to get to school the next morning and see whether her little scheme had worked. She felt very confident as she approached the school ground. Her horoscope had said, "Unexpected surprises and a wish come true will highlight your day." On the other hand, she knew that when she was around Joni and Crystal she had better not mention her call to David Spiegel. Her horoscope had also said, "Beware of misunderstandings with those who don't share your enthusiasm." Her two best friends definitely didn't share her enthusiasm for personally helping out Tongue-Tied.

Looking around, she didn't see either Kim or David. She did spot Joni and Crystal walking across the grass. They seemed to be deep in conversation.

She hurried to catch up with them.

"Hi, guys. What are you talking about that's so serious?" she asked cheerfully.

"Boys. What else?" answered Crystal, rolling her eyes.

Joni frowned. "Beau and I were going to go to the movies tonight, but now he wants to go *bowling*! Nobody goes bowling on Friday night. I wouldn't want to go on *any* night."

Su-Su pictured her long arms and legs getting all tangled up as she tried to run across the floor and pitch a bowling ball down an alley at the same time. It wasn't a pretty sight. She was glad Chris had never mentioned bowling to her. "Me neither," she said.

"What about you and Evan?" she asked Crystal. "Are you going bowling, too?"

Crystal laughed and her dimple immediately popped into her left cheek. "No way! We're going to the movies, except we can't agree on which one to see. The ones he likes are so gross."

Su-Su was about to say that she and Chris still hadn't discussed what they were doing that night when she spotted David Spiegel walking across campus. "Look, there's David," she said, pointing.

"So what?" asked Crystal. "You heard Tongue-Tied. She still can't get up enough nerve to say hi to him. I feel sorry for her, but what can we do?"

"Let's keep an eye on him anyway," said Su-Su. "It

was this time yesterday morning that he and Kim met on the sidewalk."

"Yeah, but she panicked and hid behind a bush," Joni reminded her.

"Wait, here she comes now," Su-Su said excitedly. "Let's see what happens when they run into each other."

Su-Su watched Kim Scarborough walking slowly toward the school. She stopped once to adjust the strap on her backpack, but as usual, she didn't talk to anyone. She didn't look around much, either. She didn't seem to notice David Spiegel leaning against the bike rack, watching her approach.

It was all Su-Su could do to keep from jumping up and down with glee. It was going to work! David was probably waiting for Kim. He definitely looked like he was going to say something to her. If he did, Su-Su knew Kim would be so thrilled that she'd never be tongue-tied again. And it was all thanks to her, Su-Su.

"I don't know why you're so determined to change her," Joni said with a sigh. "Some people are just born shy. There's nothing they can do about it. Did it ever occur to you that you might be causing even more stress in her life by pushing her into something that she doesn't feel comfortable with?"

"I'm not pushing her. She did ask for help, remember," Su-Su said. "Besides, I only left her one message so far. Look, she's almost ready to pass David and she doesn't see him yet."

Su-Su, Crystal, and Joni all focused in on Kim as she took one slow step after another in David's direction.

"I wish she'd move a little faster," said Crystal. "This reminds me of a slow-motion movie."

Suddenly Kim glanced up and a startled look came across her face. Su-Su couldn't tell if David had actually said something to the girl or she'd just noticed him standing there. Kim immediately bolted off the sidewalk and took a shortcut across the grass toward the building.

"Rats," muttered Su-Su.

"Give it up, Su-Su," said Joni. "Like I said, some people are just naturally shy."

Su-Su bit her lip. How could she explain to her friends that the more miserable Kim seemed to get, the more determined she was to help?

Chapter Eleven

Patrick was sitting in front of the television looking glum when the front doorbell rang that evening. Su-Su tiptoed past him to answer the door. She didn't want any more hassle about how he was having to miss the ball game on account of her. If the ball game was so important, why couldn't he find someone else to go with?

Chris was standing on the front porch. He looked as gorgeous as ever. His dark eyes weren't the least bit mysterious now. They were sparkling, and his sideways grin grew by a mile when he saw of her.

"Ready?" he asked eagerly.

"Yup," Su-Su answered. "I just have to tell Mom I'm leaving. Mom!" she called over her shoulder. "Chris is here!"

Mrs. McCarthy appeared in the kitchen door. She had changed from the business suit she wore as a court reporter into jeans, and her strawberry-blond hair was pulled up into a ponytail.

"Hi, Chris," she said pleasantly. "You kids have a good time, okay?"

"Thanks, Mrs. Mac," said Chris. "We won't be late."

Su-Su loved it when Chris called her mother "Mrs. Mac." It told her that he really liked her mom and felt comfortable around her. That was special.

Before she closed the door, Mrs. McCarthy waved to Chris's parents, who were sitting in the front seat of the dark green minivan idling at the curb. Su-Su had a feeling it was going to be a perfect evening. So far things were getting off to a great start.

She and Chris had been trying to decide between a comedy and a science fiction thriller playing in different theaters at Cinema Six. At the last minute Su-Su had finally convinced Chris to see the comedy.

"You wait over here while I get us some popcorn and sodas," said Chris after they had said good-bye to his parents and bought their tickets.

Su-Su nodded and watched as Chris joined an extremely long line at the concession counter. She hoped he would get served in time for them to see the beginning of the movie.

Looking around, she spotted Crystal and Evan coming in the lobby door. Crystal saw her too and waved. Then she gave a thumbs-up as she and Evan turned into the theater where a romantic movie was playing.

Su-Su chuckled. *Crystal got her way*, she thought.

Su-Su saw lots of kids she knew from school pouring into the lobby. Marissa Pauley and Todd Merrill were double-dating with Cami Petre and Marc Howe. David Spiegel came in all by himself. Dan Turpin, also known as Twister, was horsing around near the drinking fountain with Parker Hatch and Jason Duffy. They were Beau Maguire's best friends. But Su-Su couldn't spot Joni and Beau anywhere. *Poor Joni*, Su-Su thought. *She must be bowling.*

When the door opened again, Su-Su's heart jolted to a stop. Brian Ferguson was sauntering in with a couple of guys she didn't know. He hadn't seen her yet. She ducked around, turning her back to him and hoping he wouldn't notice her. She couldn't flirt with him in front of Chris!

"Hi, Su-Su," he said a moment later.

Su-Su groaned to herself. She should have known a tall girl with flaming red hair couldn't hide, even in a crowd.

She glanced back at the concession stand before answering. The line was moving slowly, and Chris's back was still to her.

"Hi, Brian," she said, unable to resist giving him a flirty smile. "Looks like everybody from school is here tonight."

"Sure does," said Brian. He was looking at her as if he wanted to say something important but couldn't quite get it out.

Su-Su glanced nervously at Chris again. Luckily, he still wasn't looking her way. If only Brian would leave! But she couldn't just tell someone as cute as Brian Ferguson to get lost. She didn't want to either.

"So, uh…" he said and hesitated. Su-Su thought she saw his cheeks flush ever so slightly. "So, who did you come with tonight?"

Su-Su's mouth froze in a half smile. Why did he want to know? Was he going to suggest that they sit together? A tiny thrill raced through her. She couldn't help imagining for an instant what it would be like to be on a date with Brian.

He was waiting for an answer, and Su-Su knew she couldn't lie. "Chris Oberlin," she said softly. She also knew she was doomed. Brian would never talk to her again now that he knew she was dating Chris. The two of them probably knew each other. After all, they were in the same first-period class.

Brian thought a moment and then shook his head. "Chris Oberlin? The name sounds familiar, but I guess I don't know her," he said. A grin broke across his face as he turned to rejoin his friends. "Maybe I'll see you later."

"Yeah. Later," Su-Su said numbly. She couldn't believe it. The name Chris was given to both boys and girls, and Brian thought she had come with a girl!

"Hey, wake up! Have I been gone that long?"

It was Chris. To Su-Su's amazement he was standing beside her, holding a cardboard tray with a giant tub of popcorn and two soft drinks on it.

Su-Su laughed self-consciously. "Whoops! Guess I spaced out for a while."

Out of the corner of her eye she saw Brian and his friends heading for the same movie she had convinced Chris to see. What was she going to do now? She'd die if she walked down the aisle with Chris and Brian realized that Chris was a boy. She couldn't take a chance on doing anything that would make her lose Chris!

Desperate, she plastered a goofy grin on her face. "You know what, Chris? I changed my mind. I'd rather see that sci-fi flick after all."

Chris looked puzzled. "I thought you hated movies like that."

Su-Su shrugged. "I thought I'd expand my horizons. I bet it'll be great."

The previews had started by the time they made

their way down the dark aisle and found seats. They nibbled on the popcorn, and when the tub was empty, Chris pushed it under his seat and slipped an arm around Su-Su. She snuggled close and settled in to watch the movie. Maybe it wouldn't be too awful.

The trouble was, she couldn't get into the story. Instead of the characters lost on a strange planet, she kept seeing Brian Ferguson's face.

Oh, no! Su-Su thought. A horrible realization was beginning to dawn on her. She was crazy about Chris—but now she had a crush on Brian too!

Chapter Twelve

The next morning Su-Su dragged herself out of bed and surveyed the tangle of bedclothes. Her blanket hung over the side. One of her pillows was on the floor. It had been a terrible night. She had tossed and turned, worrying about the incredible predicament she was getting herself deeper and deeper into.

How can I like two boys at once? she asked herself for the hundredth time. This was driving her crazy!

Su-Su stared at herself in the dresser mirror and made a face. "I'm a *flirt,* that's how," she whispered to herself. "I know I got carried away, but it was so much fun. And so easy."

She dropped back down on her bed and thought about Tongue-Tied. Why wasn't Tongue-Tied the one who was flirting instead of her? David Spiegel was at the movie last night. If Kim had taken Su-Su's advice, she might have been there with him.

Su-Su sighed. Maybe if she concentrated on helping Kim and David get together, she could forget about her own problems for a while.

I'll call David again, she thought. *And I'll disguise my voice so he'll think it's someone different than the one who called him before.*

She started practicing voices. "Hi, David. You don't know me, but I'm a friend of Kim's," she said in a high-pitched voice.

Su-Su shook her head. She sounded like a little kid. *Maybe I can do April Mathis*, she thought. She had done that once on Boy Talk, and everyone had fallen for it. If David thought a popular girl like April was interested in getting him and Kim together, he might really listen.

She grabbed her school directory, hurried to the phone, and punched in the number. It wouldn't matter so much if David's mom answered this time because Su-Su wouldn't sound like herself.

"Hello?"

It was David!

Su-Su closed her eyes, trying to concentrate on hearing April's voice inside her head. "Hello, David," she said in her best April voice.

"Who's this?" David asked. He sounded as if he didn't care that much.

"You mean you don't recognize my voice?" asked

Su-Su, faking surprise. "I thought everyone knew me at school."

"Well, I don't," David said grumpily.

"Never mind," said Su-Su. "What I really called about was Kim Scarborough. She's such a sweet girl, and she really has a crush on you. Well, that's all I wanted. I thought you should know. Bye."

Su-Su hung up quickly before David had a chance to say anything back. It annoyed her that he hadn't recognized April's voice. Su-Su knew she did a great April Mathis imitation.

"That wasn't enough," she murmured as she headed back to her room. "There has to be something else I can do to really get things moving. I have to *force* David to talk to Kim."

Su-Su sank down onto the rug and stared at the ceiling. Maybe she could get Kim to call David somehow. That way Kim wouldn't have to look him in the eye.

"Forget it, she'd never do that," Su-Su told herself. She stared glumly at the ceiling a little while longer. Then she sat up with a jolt. "I've got it!" she said happily. "If Kim won't call him herself, *I'll* call him and pretend I'm Kim!"

Su-Su concentrated as hard as she could. What did Kim's voice sound like? She racked her brain, but she couldn't remember.

Does she lisp? Su-Su asked herself, frowning. *Or*

have a drawl? Anything at all that I can imitate? If only she had Tongue-Tied's Boy Talk message on tape.

As hard as she tried, Su-Su couldn't think of anything in particular about Kim's voice.

"I'll just have to fake it," she told herself, heading to the phone again. "Since Kim never says anything to David, he probably doesn't know what she sounds like anyway."

Su-Su tiptoed into the hall to make sure the coast was clear. She hadn't worried about Patrick when she made her first call because it was Saturday morning, and her brother always slept in. But it was almost noon, and she couldn't take any chances on Patrick overhearing her conversation.

She was in luck. The hall was deserted.

When David answered, Su-Su took a deep breath and said in a soft, whispery voice, "Hi, David. Um...I don't know if you know me or not, but this is Kim Scarborough."

"Sure, I know you," David said. He sounded surprised. "What's up?"

"Well, I wondered if I could borrow your social studies homework from last Thursday," Su-Su asked. She had to remind herself to sound shy. "I lost mine."

"Uh, I could bring it over to your house if you want," David said

"Oh, no, that's okay," Su-Su said quickly. Things

were moving too fast here. She had to make sure everything was set up just right. "I won't be home. Why don't you give it to me before school on Monday? I always see you in the morning. Okay?"

"Sure," said David.

Su-Su took another deep breath and said as sweetly as she could, "Well, bye."

"Yeah, see you," said David.

Su-Su hung up and collapsed against the wall in relief. Not only had David fallen for it, but he had seemed pretty happy about it! That was a good sign. Correction: a *great* sign!

She had just stepped back into her room when the phone rang. It was probably Crystal or Joni, calling to talk about their dates last night.

Su-Su raced for the phone, but to her surprise, Patrick got there first. "Hello," he said thickly, rubbing sleep out of his eyes.

He listened, and a frown crossed his face. "Yeah, she's here. Who is this, anyway?"

Su-Su held her breath. Was it for her? Or her mom?

"It's for you," Patrick said. There was a funny expression on his face as he handed her the receiver. "Some guy named Brian Ferguson."

Su-Su's heart dropped. Then to her added horror, Patrick folded his arms across his chest and leaned against the wall.

Chapter Thirteen

Su-Su put a hand over the mouthpiece and scowled at her brother. "This is a private conversation. Buzz off!"

Patrick stared back at her without answering. He didn't budge, either.

Her mind was racing. She had to get rid of Patrick—*fast!*

"He's in one of my classes, okay? He's probably calling to ask about the homework assignment."

"So? Go ahead and talk to him. Forget I'm here."

And forget Chris Oberlin is your best friend, Su-Su thought frantically. *Get real.*

Su-Su could hear Brian on the other end of the line. "Su-Su? Are you there?"

She couldn't hang up on him. She would just have

to fake it the best she could. "Hi, Brian. I'm here," she said, glaring at her brother. He glared back.

"I looked for you after the movie last night. Guess I must have missed you," said Brian.

Su-Su clutched the phone. "Yeah...well..." she faltered. She didn't know what to say with Patrick listening.

"And you know what else?" asked Brian.

"No, what?" Su-Su asked. She was getting desperate. She didn't know how long she could keep saying things that wouldn't make Patrick suspicious.

"I've been trying to figure out who Chris Oberlin is. I *know* I've heard her name around school. What does she look like, anyway?" asked Brian.

Su-Su's knees went weak with relief. Brian still hadn't figured out that Chris was a guy and that he was in Brian's first-period class! Su-Su had a feeling she'd be in serious trouble soon, but she had to keep up with the lie. *Not a like, exactly.* Su-Su thought.

"Well, let's see. Dark hair and eyes...um...just, you know, regular," she said.

Patrick let out a bored sigh. Su-Su hoped that meant he was losing interest. As if to answer her silent prayer, he yawned and went back into his room, closing the door.

Saved! Su-Su thought, almost leaping with joy. *I have an out now!* She could just tell Patrick that Brian was calling to ask her about a girl she knew.

Her brother had only heard Su-Su's side of the conversation. He would have to believe her.

But what will happen on Monday? she remembered with a start. Brian's first-period teacher would call the roll and a guy would answer to the name Chris Oberlin!

"Are you still there?" Brian asked.

"Yeah, I'm still here," she said. "So how'd you like the movie last night?"

"Oh, man! It cracked me up, " Brian answered. "Did you see that one, too?"

"No, lucky you. We saw—I mean, *I* saw a stupid sci-fi flick," replied Su-Su.

"I hate sci fi," said Brian.

Su-Su smiled to herself. She and Brian had something in common, but she didn't dare mention that. He might ask why she went to see a science fiction thriller in the first place if she didn't like them.

"You know," Brian began slowly. He hesitated a moment, then said, "I wouldn't mind seeing that movie I saw again. Would you like to go tonight? With me?"

Su-Su wanted to die. If only she could say yes! She'd love to go out with him.

But I can't! she told herself sternly. Thinking fast, she said, "Gosh, I'd really love to, but I've already invited some friends over for a sleepover."

"Yeah? Oh, well, I guess you couldn't just go off to

a movie with me and leave them at your house, huh?"

Su-Su knew he was trying to make a joke, but she could definitely hear disappointment in his voice.

"No, I guess I couldn't," she said. "Too bad."

"Hey, I know! I could come over. Maybe bring some guys."

Su-Su groaned to herself. Could this whole thing get any worse? "That'd be really fun," she said quicky, "but my mom won't let me have guys over when I'm having a slumber party." This time she wasn't lying. That was one rule Mrs. McCarthy was incredibly strict about.

"Sure. Well, guess I'd better go," said Brian, sounding disappointed again. "See you around, okay?"

"Okay. Bye. And Brian," she couldn't resist adding, "I'm glad you called."

Su-Su heard the dial tone on the line and slowly dropped the receiver into the cradle. She glanced at Patrick's closed bedroom door, hoping that he hadn't been eavesdropping. She wouldn't put it past her brother.

Back in her own room, Su-Su ran through the whole conversation in her head. Why had she led Brian on like that? It wasn't fair to him at all. She had even told him she was glad he called. Now he would probably call again. And Patrick might answer the phone again. And he would run straight to Chris.

"How could I mess this up so much?" she asked herself miserably. Things were getting *way* too complicated.

Chapter Fourteen

"So did you and Beau really go bowling last night?" Crystal asked when she, Su-Su, and Joni settled into Su-Su's room for a last-minute slumber party that evening. Su-Su was only half listening to the conversation. Her mind was on her own problems.

"We sure did," Joni said, rolling her eyes. "And you know how many pins I knocked down in the entire first set? Eleven! It was disgusting. I *hate* bowling."

Crystal giggled. "You only hit eleven pins? You get ten chances to hit ten pins and you only got *eleven* altogether? That's pathetic!" Then she gave Joni a sympathetic look and added, "Just kidding."

"So what did you guys do last night?" asked Joni.

"Evan and I went to see the best movie," Crystal

said. "It was so romantic. He won't admit it, but I think he liked it as much as I did."

Joni looked at Su-Su. "You're awfully quiet tonight. Did you and Chris have a fight?"

Su-Su shook her head. She wasn't sure she could talk around the tears welling up in her throat. But she had to talk to somebody, and Joni and Crystal were her best friends. But what would they think of her if she told them the truth? She didn't want to take the chance.

She cleared her throat. "Chris and I went to see that science fiction thriller I was telling you about. And it was the worst."

"I thought you had him convinced to see the comedy," said Crystal.

"I did, but..." She hesitated. "I decided to see the one Chris wanted to see for a change. We always do what I want to do." She looked away.

"That's not the whole story, is it?" Joni asked softly. "Come on, Su-Su. If something's wrong, you can tell us."

Su-Su took a deep breath. "I know, guys. It's just that..." She felt the tears clogging her throat again. It was no use trying to hide her problem from her best friends. Besides, she needed their advice.

Finally she said, "Okay, here goes. Joni, you were right when you accused me of flirting with that cute boy on the beach. I wasn't trying to cheat on Chris, honest. I just wanted to try out the techniques in that magazine article. I was kind of surprised, but they worked—at least the ones I tried did."

She paused, trying to find the right words to explain.

"Then I saw him at school, and he actually came up to *me*! I realized that I could get some valuable fliritng experience that I could pass on to Tongue-Tied."

Su-Su paused again and shook her head. "No, that's not really the truth. He's so cute. I loved flirting with him."

"I can't believe you'd do that," said Joni. "I thought you were crazy about Chris."

"I am," Su-Su insisted. "It's just that flirting was so easy. The most important thing was keeping Chris from finding out."

"Uh-oh," said Crystal, looking worried. "Did he?"

"No," said Su-Su. "Not yet, anyway." She told her friends about talking to Brian in the lobby while Chris was buying popcorn and how Brian thought Chris was a girl.

"So that's why I changed my mind about which movie to see. I didn't want us all to end up in the same theater. And there's one more thing. Brian called me this morning and asked me out for tonight. I wanted to tell him about Chris, but I couldn't. I told him I was having a slumber party tonight."

Joni shook her head. "Wow. I don't think you're taking all of this very seriously, Su-Su McCarthy. What about Chris? What if he gets hurt?"

"He won't! He can't! I mean, I really *like* him. It's just that..." Su-Su looked from Crystal to Joni. It was time for the big confession. "I think I have a crush on both of them now."

Crystal winced. "Ouch! You're in trouble big-time. What are you going to do?"

"That's why I need your help," Su-Su said, sighing. "I don't know *what* to do. I really like Brian, but every time I think of breaking up with Chris to go out with him, I know I can't do it."

"Well, that only leaves one other choice," said Joni.

"What's that?" Su-Su asked hopefully.

Joni put a sympathetic arm around Su-Su's shoulders. "You're going to have to level with Brian."

"I can't do that!" Su-Su wailed.

"You have to," Joni said solemnly. "I mean, he'll find out eventually that Chris is a boy and that you guys are dating. Isn't it better if he hears it from you first?"

"I'm with Joni," said Crystal. "It'll be hard, Su-Su, but it's the only thing you can do."

Su-Su thought about school on Monday and that first-period roll call. She knew her friends were right.

"It's going to be really hard," she said softly. "I mean, what am I going to say?"

"It's really up to you," said Crystal. "But you know you'll always have me and Joni to lean on, no matter what."

"Yeah," said Joni. "We won't ever let you down." she chuckled softly. "At least you didn't get messed up in poor Tongue-Tied's problems."

Su-Su felt herself stiffen.

Joni looked at her in alarm. "You didn't, did you?"

"Well, just a little," Su-Su said, looking anxiously at her friends. "I called up David Spiegel and pretended I was Kim. I asked him to loan her some homework Monday morning at school. I thought it would finally get them together. I guess I shouldn't have done that, huh?"

Crystal and Joni looked sadly at Su-Su. Neither of them said a word.

Chapter Fifteen

Su-Su left for school on Monday morning knowing that two major things were about to happen. David Spiegel would offer his homework to Kim Scarborough, and a big romance would blossom. That was the good thing. The bad thing was, she was going to have to face Brian and tell him she already had a boyfriend.

She had thought about both boys all night and she was sure now that it was the right thing to do. She had a crush on Brian, but Chris was the boy she liked best. She didn't even know Brian, anyway, and she certainly could never cheat!

Crystal and Joni were waiting by the front steps when she got to school.

"You're going to talk to Brian right away and get it

over with, aren't you?" asked Joni.

Su-Su hesitated.

"You really should do it now," said Crystal. "It'll only get harder the longer you put it off."

"But I haven't figured out what to say yet," Su-Su protested.

Joni shook her head. "If you haven't thought of anything by now, you never will."

Su-Su bit her lower lip and looked around. Brian was nowhere in sight. But she did see David Spiegel crossing the street.

"Hey, guys, here comes David," she said excitedly. "I can't go look for Brian now. I have to see what happens when David gives Kim the homework."

Joni put a hand on her hip and gave Su-Su a look of disgust. "Forget David and Kim. You've got more important things to take care of."

"But—" Su-Su began.

"Joni and I'll keep an eye on them and tell you what happens," said Crystal. "Go on," she urged. "You'll feel better when it's over."

Su-Su sighed. She knew her friends were right. Her scalp was tingling as if a thousand butterflies were playing in her hair. But she had to get it over with before she lost her nerve.

She found Brian at the drinking fountain in the hall beside the office. He hadn't seen her yet, and she couldn't help thinking how great he looked. He probably played volleyball at the beach every day to keep that gorgeous tan.

Just then he looked her way, and a smile instantly lit up his face when he saw her.

"Hi, Su-Su," he called, waving her over. "How'd the slumber party go?"

"Fine," she said. "It was no big deal. Just me and my two best friends."

"I hope you didn't talk about me," he teased.

Su-Su knew the perfect moment had arrived. She had to get the words out. "As a matter of fact, we did. I told them how nice you are and how much I like you...as a friend."

Brian looked surprised. Su-Su quickly began talking again before he had a chance to say anything.

"There's something you need to know. I didn't exactly tell you the truth about Chris Oberlin. He's a guy, not a girl."

For a moment Brian's face was blank. "You mean... he's your boyfriend?"

Su-Su nodded. "I know I should have told you the truth before, but, well, I like you, too. But I've been thinking it over. I don't want to break up with Chris and I don't want to cheat on him. You probably think I'm a terrible person for doing this to you. I'm really sorry."

There. She'd said it. The whole time she'd been talking, she had been avoiding Brian's eyes. Now she looked straight at him. Her heart lurched at the disappointment in his eyes.

"Oh, hey, that's okay. Well, not exactly *okay*," he added shrugging. "I mean, I'm sorry, too. I really hoped we could go out sometime. But thanks, Su-Su."

Su-Su looked at him in surprise. "For what?"

"For telling me the truth," he said. This time he smiled at her.

She sighed with relief. "It felt awful to be living a lie."

Brian glanced at his watch. "Hey, it's almost time for the bell. I'd better hit my locker if I'm going to make it to class on time."

"Me, too," Su-Su murmured.

"Well," Brian said. Su-Su had the feeling he didn't really want to leave. "Guess I'll be seeing you around."

"Sure. See you."

Su-Su watched him disappear into the crowd. She did feel better. But in a way she felt worse. It was awful to choose between two guys. On the other hand, she could hardly wait to see Chris again. They were perfect together, and she was crazy about him!

As she turned to head for her own locker, Su-Su had the feeling that someone was watching her. She glanced around quickly, locking eyes with Chris. He looked angry.

Su-Su gasped. How long had he been standing there? He had obviously seen her talking to Brian. Why would he look so mad otherwise?

"Hi, Chris!" she called out in a voice an octave higher than normal.

Chris didn't answer. Instead he turned around and stormed off down the hall.

Chapter Sixteen

Su-Su raced after Chris, ducking and dodging around kids milling around in the halls. Once she got stuck behind a group of slow-moving girls and lost sight of him for a moment. Then she spotted him again and took off at full speed.

"Chris! Wait!" she called when he was in earshot. "I need to talk to you."

Chris slowed his pace and stepped to the side of the hall out of traffic. He stopped and slowly turned around to face her. The little sideways grin that she loved so much was absent, and his eyes were dark and brooding.

Suddenly Su-Su didn't know what to say. She could feel her lips trembling as she tried to find words to explain what he had just seen. Or thought he had seen.

"So it really is true," he said in a low voice.

His words caught her by surprise. "What's true?"

"The rumors." He spat out the words. "I've been hearing around school that you're hanging out with another guy. I didn't believe it. Even when I saw you talking to the same guy at the movies Friday night. And even when you acted so weird on the phone the other day. Now I know you've been cheating on me."

"Chris, it's not what you think," Su-Su began, feeling frantic.

"Yeah? And I suppose Patrick didn't answer the phone when some guy called you on Saturday, either."

Su-Su swallowed hard. Patrick had ratted, after all! But she couldn't worry about that right now. She had to concentrate on not losing Chris. She had to make him understand.

"I know it *looks* like I was flirting with someone, but actually it was sort of an experiment," she said in a rush. "See, there's this girl who's real shy around guys, and I thought that if…"

Her words trailed off as she saw Chris's mouth tighten. His eyes were filled with disbelief.

I'm doing this all wrong, she thought miserably.

"Okay, so he did ask me out, but I turned him

down," she went on hurriedly. "His name's Brian Ferguson, and you can ask him if you don't believe me. You'll see him in class right now. When you saw us talking just now, I was telling him that you were my boyfriend. You can ask him about that, too!"

Chris frowned, but he didn't say anything right away.

Please believe me, Su-Su prayed silently. *Oh, please, please!*

Chris shook his head slowly. "I don't know, Su-Su. I just don't know what to think anymore."

Su-Su watched in helpless horror as he turned away and started down the hall. Her heart was breaking.

Why did I ever read that stupid article? she thought sadly. Reaching into her backpack, she pulled out her notebook and opened it to the page where she had written down the flirting tips. Tearing out the page , she ripped it into a million tiny pieces and dropped them into the first wastebasket she passed as she headed dejectedly for class.

She was still miserable when she got to Crystal's for Boy Talk that afternoon. At lunch she had told Crystal and Joni about her conversations with both Brian and Chris. Her friends had been sympathetic, of course, but neither of them had the slightest idea about what she could do to make things right with Chris again.

She only half listened to the calls that started coming in to Boy Talk.

Beep.

"Hi, Boy Talk. There's this guy that I've liked for ages, and he used to like me, too—as a friend, I mean. That was all right with me. He used to talk to me a lot. You know, horse around with me and my friends, stuff like that. But now he's stopped, and whenever I go up to him and say something, he clams up. I really want him to like me again. What should I do? This is Former Friend."

"How stupid," muttered Su-Su. "Who needs a friend like that?"

She barely listened as Joni and Crystal talked over Former Friend's problem.

"If you ask me, she's lucky," said Joni. "I hate it when guys horse around."

Crystal looked thoughtful. "Or maybe he's just discovered he really likes her , and he's having trouble handling it."

Beep.

"I hope you don't think my problem is dumb, Boy Talk, because I think it's pretty serious. My boyfriend and I have been seeing each other for almost a month. Trouble is, he's a jock. When he's not playing ball, he's watching sports on TV. Now he says he can't go out with me until the season's over, and he wants me to wait for him and not date anyone else. I like him a lot, but it's a long time until the end of the season. What should I do? Call me On the Sidelines."

Su-Su paced the floor, wishing the hour would be over.

The next few calls were just kids phoning in to listen. Su-Su sighed wearily when someone began recording a message a few minutes later.

Beep.

"Hi, this is a message for On the Sidelines. Let him take time out if he wants to, but there's no reason for you to do the same thing. Let him know that you're a good sport and would like to date him again after the season *if* you haven't joined another team. Call me No Time-outs."

"Wow, that was good advice," said Joni. "Don't you think so, Su-Su?"

Su-Su was about to say that she couldn't care less when the phone rang again.

Beep.

"This is Tongue-Tied, but I'm not feeling very Tongue-Tied right now. I'm steaming! Today at school I saw a girl who already *has* a boyfriend flirting with the boy I like. And a boy I *hate* won't leave me alone. He even tried to give me his homework this morning before school. Can you believe it? What am I doing wrong?"

Su-Su stared at the answering machine, her mind

spinning. Was *she*, Su-Su, the one who had been wrong? Maybe David Spiegel wasn't the boy Kim Scarborough had a crush on.

Could it have been Brian Ferguson Tongue-Tied had been talking about all along?

Chapter Seventeen

"Oh, my gosh! We forgot to tell you," cried Crystal. "When David went up to Kim at school this morning and tried to give her his homework, she wouldn't even talk to him! She just gave him a dirty look and ran into the building."

"It happened just after you went in to look for Brian. Kim couldn't have been far behind you," said Joni.

"You're kidding," Su-Su groaned. She had been so wrapped up in her own problems that she'd totally forgotten the big meeting she had set up between Kim and David.

"I guess whenever we saw Kim avoiding David, it wasn't because she was shy," said Joni. "She just doesn't like him."

"But she really is shy," Crystal pointed out. "We all know that."

Joni tapped her chin. "Who do you suppose the guy is she really likes?"

"That's what I want to know. And Tongue-Tied said she saw another girl flirting with him today," mused Crystal. "A girl who...already has a boyfriend," she added thoughtfully.

"And she went into the school right after you did, Su- Su," added Joni.

Su-Su's heart stood still as Crystal and Joni both looked at her. "Brian Ferguson?" they asked in unison.

"That's what I was thinking, too," Su-Su admitted. "I mean, I *was* talking to him this morning before class, only I wouldn't exactly call it flirting."

"Maybe it was just that way to Kim," said Joni. "She's too shy to even look him in the eye. Remember? "

"But it could still be somebody else. Actually, it could be almost anybody else." Su-Su added hopefully. "Just think of all the guys there are at school and how many of them must have talked to a girl sometime today. It's probably just a coincidence that we all immediately thought of Brian."

Crystal giggled. "Hey, Su-Su, it's Chris," she teased. "You talked to *him* today, too."

"Come on, guys," begged Su-Su. "You know I

don't want Tongue-Tied's crush to be Brian. It's partly because I'm sorry I messed everything up for her. I mean, I really wanted to help."

"What's the other part?" Crystal asked slyly.

Su-Su felt her face go red, but she ignored the question.

"Admit it," said Joni. "You may have turned Brian down, but you still like him, don't you?"

"I don't know," Su-Su said dejectedly. "I'm so confused. First I told Brian I wouldn't go out with him, and then Chris acted as if he wants to break up. I could end up with nobody!"

Beep.

"Hi, Boy Talk," said a familiar voice.

"April!" screeched Su-Su. "What does she want *now?*"

"I just heard the message from Tongue-Tied, and I have a question for her. I don't know if this has anything to do with your problem or not, Tongue-Tied, but I did see Su-Su McCarthy falling all over Brian Ferguson this morning. And guess what? He's not her boyfriend! Just call me Watchful."

"That miserable gossip!" Su-Su shrieked. "As if I don't have enough trouble! What does she have against me, anyway?"

"Probably nothing," said Joni. "She just likes to mess in other people's lives. *And* Boy Talk. It makes her feel important."

"Well, she can leave me alone," Su-Su muttered. She sat down hard in a chair beside the desk, dropping her head into her hands. "I need this, guys. I really need this right now."

Fortunately April's call was the last of the day. Su-Su watched numbly as Crystal took out the Boy Talk tape and replaced it with her father's tape. Suddenly Su-Su realized that Joni hadn't said a word for ages. She was gazing out the window as if she were in a fog.

"What are you thinking about, Joni?" Su-Su asked cautiously.

Joni turned around. "I just might be having a moment of brilliance."

"What now?" Su-Su asked wearily. She had had just about all the excitement she could stand for one day.

Joni bounded across the room. "Listen to this!" she said. "One way to get April, Kim, *and* Chris—all three of them—to believe you weren't flirting with Brian is to fix up Brian and Kim. If you could pull that off, they would think you're a caring person instead of a cheating one."

"A cheating one!" Su-Su said indignantly.

"That's just what they think!" Joni hurriedly assured her. "You know I'd never think that about you."

"Joni has a point," said Crystal. "Chris couldn't be

—86—

mad at you if he thought you were just playing matchmaker, right. And April wouldn't have anything to gossip about so she'd probably shut up for a while. In fact, she'd look really stupid."

"Not to mention how Kim would feel," added Joni. "It just might work."

"Okay, okay," said Su-Su, holding up her hands in protest. "I get the point. I just need to think about this a little bit."

It was all she could think about for the rest of the day. Was Brian Ferguson really the boy Tongue-Tied wanted? And if he was, how could she, Su-Su, possibly get them together?

And if she did, how would *she* feel?

Chapter Eighteen

By the next morning, Su-Su had convinced herself that the boy Kim Scarborough liked couldn't possibly be Brian. And not just because she didn't want him to be, either. The whole thing had to have been a coincidence. To prove it to herself, she was going to walk up to Kim before school and strike up a conversation. If Kim was nice to her, she'd know it wasn't Brian, and that would settle the question once and for all. But what if she *wasn't* nice? Su-Su didn't want to think about that possibility.

Su-Su told her plan to Crystal and Joni as soon as they got to school.

"Isn't that a little risky?" asked Crystal. "I mean, if Brian is the guy she likes and she won't talk to you, how are you going to get her to let you fix her up?"

"I'll think of something," Su-Su said, sighing. "Listen, I'm going to wait here for her. When she comes by, I'll just say hi. I'll tell you at lunch what happens."

Su-Su tried to act calm as she leaned against a palm tree and waited for Kim. She looked at her watch a few times, starting to worry that Kim wasn't coming to school that day, when she saw her approaching.

Su-Su took a deep breath and stepped away from the tree when Kim came up. "Hi, Kim!" she said brightly, trying to sound friendly.

Kim raised her brows. "What do *you* want?"

Su-Su's optimism evaporated. There wasn't much question that Kim wasn't glad to see her. She cleared her throat nervously. "Oh, nothing much. Last year we had a class together, but I haven't seen much of you this year." She shrugged. "Just thought I'd say hi."

Kim set her jaw firmly, anger clouding her face.

Su-Su was about to quit in defeat. It was definitely Brian that Kim wanted. And Crystal had been right. There was no way she could help Kim as long as Kim stayed mad at her. Still, Su-Su knew Kim was hurting inside. She couldn't let herself give up without one more try.

Just then she saw April Mathis and Molly Triola walk by. They stopped for a second and glanced back at Su-Su and Kim.

Su-Su tried not to look back, but she couldn't help it. Sure enough, April was smirking. Now April knew she'd been right about Su-Su, and she would probably spread more gossip all over school by lunch time. Chris might hear it, and then he'd believe he'd been right about her, Su-Su, after all.

That does it! Su-Su thought angrily. She turned back to Kim. There was one thing she could do.

"You know, I listen to the messages on Boy Talk sometimes," said Su-Su.

Interest flickered in Kim's eyes, but her angry expression didn't change.

"You're Tongue-Tied, aren't you?" Su-Su asked softly.

Kim's rigid face seemed to crumple, and tears formed in her eyes. "What do you want with Brian, anyway?" she asked in a voice just above a whisper. "You already have Chris Oberlin."

Su-Su bit her lip and tried to think of something to say. She couldn't tell Kim that she was only practicing her flirting techniques when she met Brian. Kim would hate her even more for being so successful at something she couldn't bring herself to do. And Su-Su certainly couldn't tell Kim that she was researching ways to help Tongue-Tied. Kim would feel even more like a loser.

"You know, the only time I'm ever around Brian is when a bunch of us play volleyball at the beach. He hardly even notices me," Kim huffed. "I'm sure now that *you've* got him wrapped around your little finger he'll forget I even exist."

"That's not true!" Su-Su cried. Then she stopped. "Volleyball?" she whispered. Why hadn't she seen the connection before?

"Kim, that's it!" she said excitedly.

Kim eyed her suspiciously. "What's it?"

"Don't you see?" Su-Su began. "Wait a minute, let's back up. First of all, I admit to flirting with Brian. Okay? I won't try to explain it all right now. It's a long story, and I know you won't believe me if I tell you that I really wanted to help you. But when you saw me talking to Brian yesterday in the hall, I wasn't flirting. Honest. I was telling him that I already have a boyfriend."

She paused, and Kim seemed to relax a little.

"So here's the good part," said Su-Su. "You can make Brian notice you if you remember something very important: breaking the ice is the first step to melting his heart. You can start talking to Brian about *volleyball!* You both love to play, and it's easy to talk about something you have in common—even when you're shy."

Su-Su was suddenly aware that Kim was staring at her. "You're Icebreaker, aren't you?" Kim asked in astonishment. "You called in to Boy Talk and gave me that same advice."

Su-Su caught her breath and nodded.

"Then you really *were* trying to help," said Kim.

Su-Su felt a stab of guilt. She hoped she never had to admit to Kim about her own crush on Brian and about her encouragement of David Spiegel.

"Yeah, I really was," Su-Su said around the lump that was forming in her throat.

Kim sighed. "But you don't understand how it feels to be shy. You've probably never been shy in your life."

Su-Su was about to agree with Kim. Then she remembered how she used to feel around Chris when Patrick first started bringing him home. Her heart had swelled up inside her like a giant balloon, choking off her breath and making it impossible for her to speak.

"You'd be surprised," she said, grinning. "I think most girls know how it feels to be shy around a boy they really like."

Kim looked at Su-Su as if she wanted to believe her.

"Why don't you give to give it a try? Ask him when the next volleyball game is going to be. That's all you have to do. He'll tell you and then he'll probably ask you if you're going to play."

"What then?" Kim asked anxiously. "What if I tell him I'm playing? What should I say next?"

Su-Su breathed a silent sigh of relief. It sounded as

if Kim was going to give it a try! "There are lots of things you can do. I have a whole list of them at home."

A smile lit up Kim's face. "Will you give me some coaching?"

"You bet I will," said Su-Su, grinning back at Kim. "Let's talk about it on the way to our lockers. It's almost time for the bell."

They walked slowly toward the school building, discussing the flirting tips. Su-Su felt great. In spite of all her mess-ups, she was actually going to help Kim take a big step toward getting over being Tongue-Tied.

Su-Su felt even better as she and Kim climbed the front steps to the school a couple of minutes later. April and Molly were staring at them with flabber-gasted looks on their faces.

Chapter Nineteen

Even though Su-Su felt great about helping Kim, she still hadn't solved her own problem with Chris. She saw him twice in the halls between classes that morning, and both times he ignored her.

"I think I've lost him, guys," she told Crystal and Joni at noon. She took a tiny nibble out of her tuna sandwich. It tasted awful. She could barely swallow it.

"You're not going to just give up, are you?" Joni asked indignantly. "There's got to be something you can do."

"Have you thought about talking to Patrick?" asked Crystal. "He's Chris's best friend. Maybe he could help you out."

Su-Su rolled her eyes. "He's done enough damage

already. Besides, it would be way too embarrassing. Patrick and I don't always mean all the things we say to each other, but still, I don't want him to know that much about my private life." Then another thought popped into Su-Su's mind. "What will I do if Chris breaks up with me and still comes over to see Patrick? I'll *die!*"

"Maybe he won't break up with you," Crystal said. "You just have to talk to him. Why don't you call him or catch him in the hall?"

"I've already tried to talk to him. He wouldn't listen," Su-Su said. "If I tried again and he still ignored me, I'd be totally humiliated. I'd never be able to face him again."

The three girls lapsed into gloomy silence.

Su-Su put her tuna sandwich back in her lunch bag. If only there was some way to go back in time and do things differently—but of course there wasn't. She was stuck with the consequences of what she had done, and she couldn't change that.

Suddenly she felt a tap on her shoulder. Turning, she was surprised to see Kim Scarborough standing there, looking nervous. She was holding a lunch tray containing the remnants of a hamburger and fries.

Kim swallowed hard and said, "Can I talk to you a minute, Su-Su?"

"Sure," said Su-Su. Then she brightened. "Did you do it? Did you talk to Brian?"

Kim shook her head. "Not yet. But I'm finished with my lunch, and he's almost finished, too. We'll both have to take our trays back to the tray return. I was thinking about—" She froze, and her eyes filled with terror. "I can't do it," she said, shaking her head. "I just can't."

Su-Su thought a minute. "Don't you love to play volleyball?" she asked.

Kim nodded mutely. Her eyes were still big and frightened.

"And aren't you dying to find out when there's going to be another game?"

Kim nodded again and darted a quick look across the lunch room.

"Is there anybody in this cafeteria you could ask when the next game is?" Su-Su asked. "You know, just run up to them and tap them on the shoulder the way you did with me just now?"

"I could do that," Kim said. "In fact I'll do it right now."

Su-Su watched as Kim set her tray down on Su-Su's table and zigzagged through the crowded room. She stopped behind Brian, who had just reached the tray return. Kim took a deep breath and looked questioningly back at Su-Su, as if to ask if she should really go through with it.

Su-Su nodded vigorously. "Go ahead," she mouthed.

"What's going on?" asked Joni.

"Shhhh!" said Su-Su. "I think Kim's getting ready to break the ice."

She held her breath as Kim tapped Brian on the shoulder. He looked around and smiled. Su-Su's heart jolted. He was looking at Kim the same way he had looked at *her* at the beach.

It seemed to Su-Su that the two of them kept talking for ages. She tried to take another bite of her tuna sandwich, but she just couldn't force it down.

Suddenly Kim was standing beside the table again.

"Guess what?" she said excitedly when Su-Su looked up. "There's a game after school today. And guess what else? He said he hopes I'll be there because I'm such a great player! Do you think it worked?" She looked at Su-Su anxiously.

"Yup," said Su-Su. "I also think you're going to have to change your name. Tongue-Tied's not going to fit anymore. Hey, you can have my name!"

A grin spread across Kim's face. "Icebreaker, huh?" she said.

"You got it," said Su-Su.

"Thanks, Su-Su," said Kim. "You've been great."

Su-Su watched Kim leave the cafeteria, feeling mixed emotions. No matter what happened with her and Chris, Brian was probably out of the picture. "I guess I should be glad I could help out Tongue-

Tied," she said to her friends.

Crystal gave Su-Su a sympathetic look. "That's what Boy Talk's all about, right?"

"Besides, you haven't lost Chris yet," added Joni.

Su-Su shrugged sadly and glanced around the cafeteria. The crowd was dwindling as kids finished their lunches and headed outside for the rest of the period. As her eyes swept the room, they locked with another pair of eyes, staring straight at her.

Chris!

Su-Su turned quickly away. She couldn't take rejection right now. "Come on, guys, let's get out of here," she murmured.

She stuffed the rest of her lunch trash into the bag, drained the last drops of milk out of the carton, and then stood up. Crystal and Joni were already moving away from the table.

Su-Su couldn't help wondering if Chris was still watching her. What was he thinking? Was he planning how to tell her he wanted to break up? She shivered at the thought. What would she say back? What *could* she say? But when she looked in his direction again, he was gone.

Sighing, she followed her friends through the door and out into the hall.

"Hey, Su-Su, I need to talk to you."

Startled, Su-Su looked around to see Chris standing beside the drinking fountain. He had a serious expression on his face, but at least he didn't look mad.

"We'll go on outside," Joni told her.

"Right. We'll wait for you by the bike rack," said Crystal.

Su-Su headed slowly toward Chris. Her lips felt numb. Her palms were sweaty. Her heart was pounding, and butterflies were zooming around in her stomach. *All the same things Tongue-Tied must have gone through when she came face-to-face with Brian.*

Chris looked down at the floor, and Su-Su's agony grew. It was obvious that he was getting up his nerve to break the bad news to her. She wished he would quit stalling and get it over with.

"What is it?" she asked fearfully.

Slowly Chris's eyes rose to meet hers. "I don't know how to say this," he began. "I just…"

He dropped his gaze again, and Su-Su could feel her heart shattering into a million tiny pieces.

Finally he blurted out, "I'm sorry I didn't believe you before."

"What?" gasped Su-Su.

Chris looked embarrassed. "I said, I'm sorry I didn't believe you. It's just that, well, I heard all those rumors and saw you talking to Brian Ferguson. What was I supposed to think?"

Su-Su stared at him openmouthed. "So you believe me now?" she asked.

Chris nodded. "Especially after I saw you talking to Kim Scarborough before school this morning. She's pretty shy, and you said something about trying to help out a girl who was shy."

He paused, shifting uneasily from one foot to the other.

Su-Su held her breath.

"And I remembered that you said I should talk to Brian if I didn't believe you," Chris went on. "So I did. He said he was real disappointed when you told him you were going out with me. I felt like a jerk. I should have trusted you in the first place. Su-Su, I really like you a lot."

Su-Su's heart soared. "I forgive you for not believing me," she said, giving him a huge smile.

Chris gave her the little sideways grin she loved. Things were going to be okay! This was one blissed-out day.

Hi, guys! This is Crystal. Hope you liked Tongue-Tied. *Here's a sneak peek at Book #6:* Crazy in Love:

"Hey, I know you! You were in my dream last night."

Joni snapped to attention. She had been daydreaming about the upcoming Valentine dance as she ambled through the halls to her next class. Now she looked around to see who had just spoken. Was someone talking to her?

To her amazement, the cutest boy she'd ever seen was looking straight at her. He had enormous green eyes, curly brown hair, and a sly smile that made her knees weak.

"Excuse me?"

"You were in my dream last night," he repeated, his grin widening. "I was at a dance and I was standing beside a girl with blond hair. You walked by and said, 'Hi, Reed.' Then you disappeared before I could find out who you were or how you knew my name. And now here you are."

"I *don't* know your name," said Joni, puzzled. "I've never seen you before in my life." She frowned. "Have I?"

BETSY HAYNES wrote her first book when she was nine years old. It was about a frog named Peppy who leaves his lily pad to see the world. Today most of her books are based on things that happened to her and her friends when they were in middle school and junior high—Betsy says she's forever thirteen!

Betsy lives on Marco Island, Florida. She and her husband, Jim, have two grown children, two dogs, and a black cat with extra toes. She enjoys traveling and spending time on her boat, *Nut & Honey*. And she really loves to talk on the phone!

WRITE TO "DEAR BOY TALK"

NEED ADVICE ABOUT

DATING? **FRIENDSHIP?** **ROMANCE?**

Joni, Crystal, and Su-Su may have an answer for you!

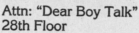

Just write to *Dear Boy Talk* at this address:

 Random House, Inc.
201 East 50th Street
New York, NY 10022

 Attn: "Dear Boy Talk"
28th Floor

Let us know what's on your mind. From secret crushes to broken hearts to major embarrassments, Boy Talk™ can help! We can't publish every letter, but we can promise to print a select few in the back of every new Boy Talk book.

Too shy to share your romance problems? Boy Talk fans can give advice for readers' problems, too! Letters began appearing in Boy Talk #2: DUDE IN DISTRESS. Just pick a problem and write to the above address—and you just might see *your* letter in print!

Dear Boy Talk:
I fell in love with a boy at first sight. He's on my uncle's basketball team and I've gone to all his practices. He lives in a different town from me, so I knew I had to do something before the season was over. There was a party at the end of the year, but I couldn't go. I asked my cousin to ask this boy to go out with me. He said, "I don't know who she is." My heart is broken. I want him to get to know me. But how?

Love at First Sight
Ohio

Dear Love:
Remember that old saying, Absence makes the heart grow fonder? The distance between you may make him seem even more exciting. And you're probably wondering what he's doing and who he's talking to all the time. Obsessing like that can drive you crazy. But how will you two get together enough to have a relationship even if he likes you, too? Maybe you should look around a little closer to home.

Crystal

Dear Love:
I agree with Crystal. And how would you know if he cheated on you? Ask your cousin to play detective and keep an eye on him? He sounds like more trouble than he's worth.

Joni

Dear Love:
I think both my friends are missing the point here. You didn't ask them for advice on planning a wedding. All you wanted to know was how to get <u>him</u> to get to know <u>you</u>, right? Maybe your cousin could invite you for the weekend, and the two of you could arrange to be somewhere he's going to be. Just walk up to him and say hi!

Su-Su

Dear Boy Talk:
I have a best friend who's always bugging me in school. We're really close, but sometimes she really gets on my nerves, especially when I'm trying to pay attention in class. I want to tell her this, but I don't want to hurt her feelings.

School Bugged
Pennsylvania

Dear Bugged:
It's great that you're so sensitive to your friend's feelings, but she needs to be sensitive to yours, too. If you don't think you can flat out tell her how you feel, try another approach. You might say that you have to listen extra hard in class from now on because you're worried you might flunk out. If she's really a good friend, she won't argue with that.

Crystal

Dear Bugged:
Sometimes you have to say it like it is. If your friend hasn't figured out by now that she should be quiet in class, someone needs to tell her. And who could do it better than her best friend. Who knows? Her grades might even improve!

Joni

Dear Bugged:
Does your friend have a motor mouth <u>outside</u> class, too? If she does, she's probably an incurable yakker, and there's not much you can do about it without hurting her feelings. Or maybe you're the one who talks all the time, and class is the only time she can get a word in.

Su-Su

Dear Boy Talk:
I have a really good friend who's a boy. We talk all the time and go to each other's houses. About a year ago, I started liking him more than a best friend. I've even asked him out, but he always says no. He says he doesn't want to mess up our friendship. What can I do?

Best Friend
Michigan

Dear Best:
That's a tough one. The big danger is that if you start dating and it doesn't work out, you could lose him completely. Is it worth taking that kind of chance?

Joni

Dear Best:
On the other hand, can you stand being in love with someone who thinks of you only as a friend? I say go for it! He already likes you a lot, or he wouldn't be your best friend. Just show him there's even more of you to like.

Su-Su

Dear Best:
I had a similar problem with my boyfriend Evan, so I know how you feel. I got lots of advice from my friends and Boy Talk, but here's what worked for me: take your time so you won't make a fool of yourself. That was a big help! Don't move too fast or he may back off and miss out on a great romance.

Crystal

Dear Boy Talk:
I want to dump my boyfriend, but I don't know how to tell him. He treats me like I don't exist. I really like him, but it just isn't working out.

Bad Dumper
Florida

Dear Dumper:
It sounds like this guy is really making you unhappy, and I agree that you should get rid of him. And I wouldn't make things worse by telling him how much you like him, either. Level with him. Let him know the way he treats you hurts. You'll feel a lot better if you do.

Su-Su

Dear Dumper:
Some guys are pretty dense. They actually think girls enjoy being treated badly. Maybe he doesn't have a clue about how you really feel. I agree with Su-Su that you should level

with him, but do it gently. If he really likes you, too, he might decide to change the way he treats you.

Joni

Dear Dumper:
Breaking up with a guy is never easy. It can hurt you as much as him. But it hurts worse to stay in a bad relationship. Make it short and get it over with. Just say, "I'm sorry, but I don't want to date you anymore." You'll feel a lot better.

Crystal

Dear Boy Talk:
My mom says thirteen is too young to wear makeup or go on dates. She says I can't do either of those things until I'm sixteen! I've tried to show her that I'm very mature, but nothing seems to work. Help!

Plain and Dateless
California

Dear Plain:
Boy, do I know where you're coming from! Sometimes my mom gives new meaning to the word overprotective. On the other hand, things are different now than when our moms were our age, and they're nervous. Would she let you go on group dates with kids she knows? Sometimes that can be more fun than going out with a guy alone! And there's a lot less pressure, too. Talk to your mom about it. Wait a while on the makeup part. If you hit her with too many things at once, she may say no to everything.

Su-Su

Dear Plain:
Su-Su has a good idea. Your mom might be even happier if you invited some kids over to your house. There are a lot of scary things in the newspaper and on TV these days. Maybe your mom just needs to get to know the kind of boys you like.

Joni

Dear Plain:
I can't really add much on the dating problem. As far as makeup goes, why don't you ask your mom to help you learn to use it? You don't want a lot of garbage on your face anyway. Ask her to help you choose soft colors that are just right for you and to show you how to apply them to look natural. She'll probably be flattered that you came to her for help.

Crystal

Dear Boy Talk:
I went out with this terrific boy last year and when he broke up with me it really hurt. Since then, I haven't been interested in anyone else, but he has had a few girlfriends. The big problem is that he still flirts with me and looks at me in a way that makes me wonder if he still likes me. What do you think I should do?

Confused
Ohio

Dear Confused:
It sounds to me as if a little serious flirting is in order. If he is interested again, I'd give him every opportunity to let you know. Start up some conversations with him. Pay him a compliment or two. (Not too many, though. The flattery might go to his head.) Let him know that you <u>might</u> be interested again, too!

Su-Su

Dear Confused:
Whoa! Don't go off the deep end and make a fool of yourself. Maybe he's just being friendly. And don't forget, guys <u>hate</u> being chased. I say, be friendly to him, but don't get carried away.

Joni

Dear Confused:
Is there anything more confusing in the whole wide world than boys? I guess that's one of the reasons we like them so much. But they can hurt us, too. Be care-

ful if he's had a bunch of girlfriends since he broke up with you. Is he the one who broke off those relationships, too? Maybe he just likes breaking hearts. You wouldn't want to set yourself up for a second one.

Crystal

Dear Boy Talk:
I have this friend who is sometimes nice to me. But she uses me by trying to get personal things out of me. When I tell her things about myself, she blabs it to all my friends. Is she a real friend?

Friend or Not
New York

Dear Friend or Not:
Not! If she were a real friend, she'd respect your privacy. And she'd value your friendship enough to keep her mouth shut. This is one friend you don't need.

Su-Su

Dear Friend or Not:
I agree with Su-Su. She doesn't have a clue as to what friendship is all about. Somebody needs to explain it to her.

Joni

Dear Friend or Not:
I think Su-Su and Joni just hit the nail on the head without realizing it. She doesn't understand what it means to be a friend. You should talk to her and tell her gently that friends care about each other and don't tell secrets behind each other's back. If she wants to be a real friend, fine. If she has to gossip, she should look for friendship somewhere else. Good luck.

Crystal

Dear Boy Talk:
I have a boyfriend who I think is very nice and caring, but he's considered a dork by a lot of popular kids. I often get made fun of because of my boyfriend. I wish

other people knew what he was really like. Why do they have to make fun of me when they don't even know him?

Caring
Michigan

Dear Caring:
I know it's hard not to let other people's opinions get to you, but who are they to judge your boyfriend? Like you said, they don't know him. Maybe you could change that. Include him in the group. After they're around him awhile, maybe they'll change their minds about him.

Su-Su

Dear Caring:
Su-Su has a good idea. Would your parents let you have a boy/girl party? Or, if you don't think he'd feel comfortable in a big group, invite a few kids over to make pizza.

Crystal

Dear Caring:
And don't forget all the good points you see
in your boyfriend. You might mention them
casually when you're talking to your friends.
And plan activities to show off any special
abilities that he has. And then watch out—
someone might try to steal him away from
you!

Joni

Remember Evil Twin's Disaster of the Day?

I hope you can help me. I've got myself in a huge mess! My twin sister is going out with the cutest guy in our school. Sometimes when he calls and I answer the phone, he can't tell if it's me or my sister (we're identical twins). Even though I know I shouldn't, I sometimes pretend I'm her and talk with him for a while. He's so sweet and we have such a great time talking that I'm starting to really like him. I think he likes talking to me, too, so now I'm wondering if I should tell him the truth. I know my sister might get mad at me, but I really like him. What should I do?

Evil Twin

Here's some advice from all you Boy Talk readers:

Dear Evil Twin:
You love your sister and like her boyfriend. Try to put yourself in her shoes. I'd sit her down and tell her everything. If she gets mad, you should say, "I'm sorry," and forget about dating her boyfriend. If she's understanding, then maybe she'll let you go out with him.

Hoping to Be Helpful
Washington

Dear Evil Twin:

Go ahead and tell him it's you. He'll at least like a girl who tells the truth and is bold enough to tell him so. Since he is the cutest boy in your school, he'll understand. Hey, if he likes your sister, then I'm sure he'll like you too. Even if your sister does get mad, deep down inside you know she'll still love you. Sooner or later, one of you will apologize.

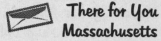
                                    There for You
                                    Massachusetts

Dear Evil Twin:

What you need to do is tell the truth. Tell your sister first. Explain why you talked to her boyfriend on the phone (he was the cutest guy in school), and why you kept it up (you started to like him). She may be mad at you, but at least she'll hear it from you first. Then speak to her boyfriend. He might like that you have an interest in him, but he might not. Also, tell him that when you started talking to him, you didn't realize it would get this far. You never know what might happen.

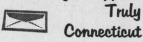
                                    Truly
                                    Connecticut

Disaster of the Day

Dear Boy Talk:
My friend and I have been friends for a long time. She was always nice to everyone and was her own person. Suddenly her life and image changed. She started hanging out with people who are a bad influence on her. They even made her steal once! I can't believe she could get pressured into that. How can I tell her she's hanging out with the wrong crowd without her going ballistic?

Mind-Boggled
Michigan

Joni   Su-Su   Crystal

Write in soon, BoyTalk readers!
Mind-Boggled needs some serious help!

PLAY

Boy Talk

EVERYONE'S-A-WINNER
GAME!

Grand Prize: An AT&T Phone
Additional Prizes: A Boy Talk Phone Card
A Boy Talk Key Chain

Details on how to claim your prize can be found on the back of your game piece insert. If the game piece is missing from your book, you can write to:

Boy Talk Game Piece
201 East 50th Street
MD 30-2
New York, NY 10022

Just send us your name and address and we'll mail you a free replacement game piece. Hurry—*offer good only while supplies last!*

Whoa! Here's another blue-ribbon series from Bullseye Books! Join the girls and horses of

Riding Academy

Jina, Andie, Lauren, and Mary Beth—the four roommates in Suite 4B at Foxhall Academy—may not see eye to eye on everything. But they do agree on one thing: they *love* horses! You'll want to read all the books in this extra-special series.